Gubblebum and The Lost Ness Monster

Peter Flint

Storm Rhino
Publishing

Childrens

Fantasy

Humour

Typeset: Size 14 Anmari

www.stormrhinopublishing.com

Cover art adapted from the "Bubble Trubble" cover created by Lily

DEDICATION

To anyone who loves stories. Stories can be: exciting, mysterious, happy, sad, serious, funny, important or just a bit of fun.

Stories are like a magic mirror. Look into it and you'll see yourself. You think, 'So, I'm not the only one who's not good at sport and scared of getting kicked or whacked with a hard ball...' 'I'm not the only one who gets into trouble for messing up my bedroom...' or 'I'm not the only one who sneaked off feeling guilty and geeky when the bully called me names...' or who thinks their ears are a bit big or wishes their hair wasn't curly. You are not the only one who doesn't get very good grades in Maths or English or is still a bit scared when your room is dark and you can hear the wind blowing outside.

Stories are like a secret door where you can peep through and see people who do things which are brave, stupid, dangerous, kind or terribly cruel...

Stories are like a space-portal or a time-machine where you can visit other towns, other cities, other lands...other planets...

A little boy was asked by a television interviewer which he like best...the film or the book about one of his favourite characters. The interviewer was surprised when he said he liked the film but the book was better. He asked him why. The little boy said, "The pictures inside my head are better..."

I hope you enjoy this story...

Gubblebum and The Lost Ness Monster

Gubblebum was bored. She had changed the baby's clothes... his fluffy sleep-suit she changed into a cuddly rabbit with a cute pink nose, white twitchy whiskers and long floppy ears. The fact that its fur was blue didn't seem to bother it a bit. It hopped and bounced around the kitchen almost knocking off a tray of toffee-apples which Gubblebum had left on the windowsill to cool. The baby gurgled and squealed with delight at its antics which saved the romper-rabbit from being changed back into a pile of dirty washing.

Suddenly the rabbit saw its reflection in a mirror. It stopped hopping and bouncing and stood admiring itself, practising whisker-twitching and nose wriggling and generally being cute. If it hadn't caught a glimpse of Pancake creeping stealthily... well as stealthily as Pancake could creep... behind it, a quick trip to the laundry-basket or being the only rabbit with bright blue fur would have been the least of its worries. It stopped its 'being cute' practice and shot out of the kitchen door closely followed by Pancake. He succeeded where the rabbit had failed and knocked the tray of toffee-apples flying up in the air. The baby chuckled and laughed...which probably saved Pancake ending up in the laundry-basket himself!

After Gubblebum had picked up the toffee-apples, wiping off as much dust and fluff as she could... the kids gobbled them so quickly they'd never notice... she changed the baby's nappy.

In a flash – well, perhaps a little longer than that – It became a pinkish-white, slithery little squid-like creature covered in pictures of Pooh... which seemed appropriate somehow. The octonappypus squelched across the kitchen floor and out into the passage. Pancake, who had given up on the romper-rabbit and come back to see if Gubblebum had left any of the toffee-apples on the floor, jumped back barking and whining as the horrid thing squirmed towards him. He pressed himself against the hall stand, bringing down on his head a shower of hats, brollies, wellies, macs and old copies of the Black Pages telephone directories which only witches could read because of the colour of the paper and the spelling. The nappy-thing sulked its way past him and dived with a splodge into the toilet. The baby began to cry.

"Like your clothes and nappy we could both do with a change," Gubblebum said, picking up the baby and giving him a hug, "Well, perhaps not quite like that." She shuddered as she thought of the Pooh-Squid.

Calvin was away for a few days. Gubble-dee-Goo flights over the forest and entertaining children at parties with balloon-animals was keeping the wolf from the door...(well, now and then Gubblebum invited him in for a cup of tea and a chat. That is, when he wasn't hanging around waiting for little girls in red outfits or running for his life from wood cutters!)

You see Calvin was so busy because Walter had called him in a panic. There had been a rush of ribbon-cutting, an overload of openings, a pile of plantings and a heap of hand-shakings in Messypotmania. The trouble was that Walter had only one pair of hands and he wasn't allowed to shake hands with both of them at the same time. He tried it once when opening a nursery school. The headmistress thought he wanted to play Ring-a-Ring-a-Roses! The Messypotmanian TV news had shown a picture of Walter, his crown over one ear, sitting on the floor holding hands with a young woman.

"Atishoo, atishoo...the Prince falls down," said the reporter. Gravellina was not amused.

"He'll need more than a tissue to wipe the tears from his eyes when I get him back in this palace!" She growled. Those people who had known her in her bossy princess days would have recognised the signs immediately and found urgent things to do...right at the other end of the palace!

Walter had offered Calvin a princely sum...which wasn't actually all that much as Walter wasn't really very good at sums...to come and help him cut ribbons, open things, plant trees and shake hands. Gubblebum had pointed out in a quiet but witchy voice that if the TV showed Calvin sitting holding hands with pretty young ladies, especially headmistresses, the dragon population of the country would increase by one hundred percent overnight...to one!

Gubblebum sniffed, "Black cats and cauldrons! The Gubble-dee-Goo's burning!" She put the baby in the playpen which began trotting around the kitchen shaking a rattle and singing nursery rhymes. She snatched the large black pot off the fire and peered into it.

"Thank covens: caught it just in time. Calvin would have been upset if there had been no Gubble-dee-Goo for little Princess Gravellinetta's second birthday party."

Saving the pan of sticky delicious Gubble-dee-Goo reminded Gubblebum of how Pancake had been chasing rabbits through the kitchen when she had been busy with a spell. The witch and the bowl of old raspberry jelly she was holding had gone flying up into the air as Pancake tried to take a shortcut to the rabbit...through Gubblebum's legs! The smelly jelly had all gone splodge into the spell and Gubblebum had gone splat into Pancake's leftover dinner.

This short flight had led to the accidental invention of Gubble-dee-Goo; Calvin's setting out to rescue the Princess Gravellina; fighting a dragon... well, sort of... the dragon turning into Prince Walter and that leading to a double Royal Wedding! All because of some old raspberry jelly... which was turning a bit green at the edges!

Gubblebum sighed. She loved Calvin, the baby and their lovely cottage at the edge of the forest. She loved all the little furry animals which came out of the trees and sat around looking cute whenever she came into the garden with the baby. She even loved the two bluebirds who insisted on fluttering around the baby's head as she walked. Several times that twittering woke him up just as she had managed to get him off to sleep... okay bluebirds were nice but they did tend to overdo it a teensy bit at times. Secretly she had to admit that she also loved Pancake although sometimes his rabbit chasing did still cause her to say a few naughty witch-words.

Her life was perfect...almost like a fairy story...well, exactly like a fairy story but that's not really so surprising is it? Why did she feel bored? She yawned.

"I think I'll sit down for a spell," she thought. "That's it!" she shouted, causing the playpen which had just rocked the baby to sleep to say, "Shhhhhhhhhhhhhhhh!" and look as annoyed as was possible for a playpen.

"I've not cast a good...or even a wicked spell for absolutely ages. When was it exactly?" Gubblebum said, "I remember turning that nasty little boy who snatched one of my toffee-apples into a snail...it was funny seeing him trying to run away...especially as the toffee-apple was about ten times as big as he was. Then there was the time when I turned Calvin's car into a car park! Come on, be serious, when was the last time I had a real wizard-sized dose of magicosity...or better still a witch-size one?" She thought hard, "Not counting the Gubble-doo-Goo...and that was an accident...the last time was at Amanda Salad's birthday party...yes that's it...when I turned all the little cucumber sandwiches into birds' beaks and they all sang 'Happy Birthday'. We had some good times together Amanda Salad and me when we were students at Hagricultural College. We've not seen each other for ages: just the usual card at Halloween wishing each other Yowltide Greetings and a Haggy New Year."

Gubblebum suddenly began to dance around the Kitchen. The playpen

shushed her so loudly that baby began
to wake up.

"Sorry," said Gubblebum.

"I should think so too," said the
playpen in a prissy voice. After
checking that the baby had gone back
to sleep Gubblebum picked up the
phone.

"Is that the witch-board? I want to
place a call to Sister Amanda Salad;
that's Baywitch 2458."

"Hello, Ms 'Manda Salad spells and
potions: charms and curses for all
occasions... no job too small... free
estimates... free delivery within five
miles. Witch service to you require?"

"Rolly, it's me: Gubblebum."

"Gubble! Fancy hearing from you. I was thinking about you yesterday...at teatime... raspberry jelly and ice cream."

"Hang on a minute Rolly...Gubble? Since when have you called me Gubble?"

"Well I know I used to call you...er...B... well something else but we're a bit older now aren't we? I mean you're a respectable married lady and a Mum and all that. Besides your Calvin's a prince and he'll be King one day and well, B...er you know just doesn't seem quite right somehow."

"Since you put it like that I suppose we've got to put on a show: Keep up appearances if only for Calvin and the baby's sake. In a way that's why I'm calling..."

"I'm sorry B...er...I mean Gubble but you've lost me...you'll have to spell it out for me. I know I can be a bit of a dimwitch at times."

"Respectable that's it spot on...since Calvin and I got married the only thing I've changed into is clean knickers. I can't remember the last time I went to a Halloween party as an angel or flew the old GTI broomstick silhouetted against the full moon... I think I've even forgotten how to cackle,"

"Oh you poor thing...how can I help?"

"It's been ages since we had a chat...it must have been at the wedding. I remember Calvin looking at me rather strangely. Well, it's not every day you see your new wife nattering to a raven. He must have thought I was raven mad...joke...raving mad. Why were you a raven?"

"Broomstick problems...you can't buy a good reliable British broomstick for spite nor money...they're not making them anymore...all foreign they are...all plastic handles and nylon bristles: when he's riding pillion the static makes poor Marmaduke's fur stick up like a hedgehog's prickles...and the names...I ask you...who's ever heard of a decent broomstick with one of them foreign names? Wanda... Muckybitsu... Toyota...I mean if you're going to have a toy broomstick you might as well get one of them brush and dustpan sets..."

"Rolly...Rolly..."

"Oh hark at me witchering on nineteen to the dozen...er...what did you ask me?"

"At the wedding...why had you changed into a raven?"

"Like I said, the blooming broomstick started making a funny noise over Dulwich and conked out over West Bromwich...good job I remembered that raven spell or it would have been flat witch. Jolly good wedding though - lots of raspberry jelly if I remember correctly. Long time no see, eh Gubble?"

"Well Rolly in a way that's why I've rung you..."

"Sorry Gubble, you've lost me..."

"I've not been to the sea for ages and well, you live by the sea...you're a sandwitch and I just wondered..."

"Of course you can Gubble old thing...come as soon as you like. Stay as

long as you like...plenty of room...just me
and old Marmaduke."

"So you've not met any woww-ee
wizards, super sorcerers or cool
conjurers?"

"Alas no: I'm still waiting for Mister
Rite to come along so a bit of company
would be great. By the way, bring the
baby and old Pancake...plenty of rabbits
around here."

Amanda Salad did look like a real
witch... no, no... not that sort: all wrinkly
and warty like a bag of prunes with the
measles. She was tall and elegant. She
had cheekbones so high that they
pushed her eyebrows into sweeping
arches. Her eyes were deep and
piercing and she made them more
dramatic with lots of mascara and
purple eye shadow tapering nearly to
the tops of her ears. Her mouth was

curved so much that it looked for all the world like a plum coloured MacDonald's sign. Her hair was long, jet black and shiny and seemed to move slowly as if someone had tipped over a large basket of snakes. She wore long tight velvet dresses in red, green or purple. Truth to tell she made Gubblebum in her leggings and baggy sweaters feel quite dull and un-witchy, and left her wishing she had fingernails three inches long painted a deep mauve...and fewer freckles!

Gubblebum staggered up the drive carrying the baby in one arm; a rucksack full of: toys, nappies, baby food, medicines on her back and a gigantic suitcase strapped to her broomstick in which were: collapsible buggies, strollers, sleepers, bouncers, feeders, bathers, shaders. There was also a thingamajig made from about twenty interlocking poles and brackets and several yards of canvas which you could click together in ten minutes or so to make...well, nobody was quite sure! Pancake trotted behind carrying nothing except his favourite toy...you've guessed it...a squeaky rubber rabbit.

After Pancake had been given his dinner and gone out looking for rabbits; the baby fed; burped; de-pooed; nappied and put into his cot for a sleep, Gubblebum and Amanda Salad sat in deckchairs each with a large cup of Witche's Brew tea and a packet of Nasty biscuits...which were not nasty at all but were made in the little town of Nasty in Southern Messypotmania.

The two witches talked and laughed about old times: spells that went wrong, broomstick rallies where they had looped the loop, bossy people they transmogrified into slugs, newts, slow worms and other crawlies and silly princesses who went round kissing frogs until their lips were all slimy and chapped and their hair full of smelly, dripping pond weed.

They were just into their third cup of Witche's Brew and Gubblebum had turned down the offer of another delicious Nasty biscuit.

"It must be absolutely magical living here by the sea," said Gubblebum, "Swimming and sunbathing in the summer and long healthy walks by the crashing waves in the winter. Lots of fresh air and all this beautiful scenery... almost makes me wish I'd taken the sand-witch course at college."

"Why didn't you Gubble?"

"Well you all seemed so, well you know, smart and posh and there was me in my jeans and sweaters. I thought I could never be a sand-witch - they're all so well bred." Gubblebum laughed, "I soon found out different. There you were with the other four on the Advanced Sand-Witch Course out all hours at parties and dances. You had a name for yourself...what was it?"

"The Slice Girls," giggled Amanda Salad. Suddenly the corners of her plum mouth turned down so that it looked almost like a purple heart. She would have burst into tears but it took her so long to make up her eyes in the morning that she had trained herself to sniff extra sadly.

"Rolly...whatever's the matter?" asked Gubblebum.

"It's my beautiful Baywitch...it's it's... (sad sniff)... it's being spoilt... (very sad sniff) by...by...by...a... (several super sad sniffs all together)"

"A what, Rolly?"

"A...a...sea-serpent...(sniff, sniff, sniff, sniffly, sniff)," Amanda Salad whispered and three large black tissues flew like bats out of a box on the table straight into her hand. She blew her nose with a loud honk which made the baby wriggle in his collapsible sleeper and Pancake lifted up his head and scratched energetically behind his ear.

"A sea-serpent! Well I know Walter had been turned into a dragon by a witch. It wasn't you by any chance was it Rolly?"

"No (sniff) it wasn't and if all I hear about that wife of his is true I'd have been doing him a favour... if it had been me of course...which it wasn't, you understand,"

"What kind of sea-serpent?" asked Gubblebum.

"Er...well...it's more of a no-see-serpent."

"A what?!"

"A no-see-sea-serpent you see."

"Rolly, that's just it - I don't..."

"You don't what?"

"I don't see."

"That's the trouble," sniffed Amanda Salad, "you can't see you see."

24

By this time Gubblebum was thoroughly confused: she felt as if she didn't know witch way to turn. "Rolly, I know you're upset but try to explain exactly what kind of sea-serpent this no-see-sea-serpent is."

Amanda Salad took a deep sniff and began. "I think there's more than one of them,"

"More than one of what...if I dare ask?"

"More than one of those no-see-sea-serpents," said Amanda Salad.

"Rolly, I know you are my oldest and dearest friend but if you do not stop going on about no-see-saw-sea-serpents I shall scream and probably turn you into something unbelievably awful like a plate of chocolate ice-cream."

"I think that sounds rather nice actually... especially if there was a little raspberry jelly..."

"Not with baked-beans and gravy it doesn't...so think very carefully before you go on Rolly or else!"

Amanda Salad gave a little sniff; then she continued quickly just in case Gubblebum began to think of ice-cream with...yuck!

"Every morning for the past two months the beautiful beach at Baywitch has been wrecked: huts smashed flat; trees uprooted; the annual sand-castle competition... trampled and...er... the ice cream stall up-ended... even the sea-side rock had been rocked onto the sand...rock's lovely you know Gubble...I mean you make all those delicious toffee-apples...but not when it's covered in sand."

Gubblebum thought of the dust and fluff on her latest batch of toffee-apples and began to feel a little sorry for Amanda Salad.

"What is causing all this damage?" she asked a little more gently.

"I've been trying to tell you before you started going on about ice-cream and gravy," she shuddered, "We all think it is a sea-serpent but no-one has ever seen it so that's why it's a no-see-sea-serpent,"

"But how do you know it's a sea-serpent if no-one has seen it?"

"The tracks, you see...every night they come out of the sea up the beach and wreck everything in sight but in the morning the no-see-sea-serpents have gone...vanished back into the sea."

"What makes you think there is more than one of these no-see-sea-serpents?"

"Well, it's the tracks you see...you don't see the sea-serpents but you do see the tracks coming from the sea...see?"

"Rolly," Gubblebum said quietly, "Baked beans... and gravy!"

"Sorry Gubble I forgot...well, some of the tracks are huge...lose a hot dog stall in them...easily...the others are smaller...but not much...we're talking disappearing deck-chairs at least...and..."

"And?" said Gubblebum, imagining enormous sea-serpents waddling from the waves.

"There are so many tracks that we think there must be at least four of them,"

"Only four? Why Rolly, that's hardly worth a witch putting on her pointy hat for. I mean to say if they were real dragons, well that might make me a bit nervous but we've all seen sea-serpents haven't we?"

"Have we?" asked Amanda Salad nervously.

"We've all seen pictures of them...as if someone's tipped a giant bowl of spaghetti hoops into the water."

Amanda Salad still wasn't sure. "But Gubble, these spaghetti hoops knock down trees...big ones and last week tipped over the band stand...solid iron that was...if that was a spaghetti hoop it certainly was powerful pasta."

"Don't you worry, Rolly," smiled Gubblebum, seeing that Amanda Salad had started to sniff again and that several black tissue bats were flapping about over the sleeping baby, "There are two of us now and I'll bet my broomstick that two witches are a match for any number of sea-serpents,"

Amanda Salad managed a weak grin, "Do you really think so, Gubble?"

"I'm sure so. Tell you what, as soon as the baby wakes up we'll take a walk along this beach of yours and see if we can think of some way to stop these invisible sea-creatures from destroying Baywitch." She had no sooner finished speaking than the baby woke up, wriggling around in his sleeper; pulling the most awful faces before opening his eyes and starting a sad little cry which meant: "I'm awake now, who's going to make a fuss of me?"

It certainly wasn't Pancake who woke from his twitching dream in which large fat rabbits ran through the forest wearing enormous heavy boots. He scratched behind his ear again; looked down his nose at the grizzling baby then set off to see if he could find a real rabbit wearing heavy boots.

It was a gorgeous afternoon as Gubblebum and Amanda Salad set off along the beach. As Amanda Salad had said, the smooth golden sand had been scraped and torn. Everywhere were huge footprints, some of which had stripy deck-chairs sticking out of them and in one especially large print the two witches could just read a sign saying: "Derek's Delicious Hot Dogs: Dash 'nd Buy One".

"Gosh, Rolly," whispered Gubblebum "I see what you mean: all this mess wasn't caused by mice."

"You can say that again," said a croaky voice.

"All this mess wasn't caused by...who on earth said that?"

"You did," said the croaky voice.

"I know I said that bit about mice but who said I could say it again? As if a witch needs permission from anyone to say anything... uh, the very idea!" said Gubblebum angrily. The two witches looked carefully around the beach. Apart from a red-haired young man wearing a cook's white apron and hat who was staring sadly into the footprint containing the hot-dog stall, the beach was deserted.

"I swear I heard someone speak," said Gubblebum.

"I should hope not," said the same croaky voice. "No swearing on this beach - it says so on that notice."

The two surprised witches looked forward for a notice and at last saw a freshly painted sign lying flat on the sand where it had been flattened by a sea-creature's giant foot. Moving nearer they read: "Do not throw stones at this notice...by order of the Baywitch Council. Anyone caught so doing will be prose...prosi...in big trubble. Signed: C Kent...Town Clock" (I think it meant Town Clerk.)

"It says nothing of the sort...about swearing, I mean," said Gubblebum.

"Never was much good at reading," said the voice, "Still, throwing stones and swearing - they're both what you'd call anti-sociabibabubble... anti-socibble... not very nice."

Gubblebum and Amanda Salad gazed in astonishment at a large untidy bird which looked something like a seagull sitting on a salt-bleached post.

"It's a seagull... a *talking* seagull... I've never heard such a thing in all my life," said Gubblebum.

"Er...Gubble...I was talking to you...at the wedding...and I was..."

"A raven, yes...but you were really in a sort of raven costume. This is a real generally non-talking seagull."

"No I'm not," said the seagull, using the pinion feathers of one ruffled wing to doff a miniature sailor's cap, "Sorry to correct a lady...er...two ladies, especially when them two ladies be witches and could turn a poor chap into a whelk or a barnacle...but what's right is right and I'm not."

"You're not right? Oh you poor thing...come to my cottage at two 'o clock on Monday and we'll discuss your problems," said Amanda Salad.

"No ladies... thanks all the same but it's not me that's not right it's... begging your pardon...you."

Gubblebum raised her arms: her eyes glowed a fiery red and little crackles of electricity began to spit from the ends of her fingers.

"Er...before you do anything you...and I...might regret your witchship, I just meant that you weren't right when you said I was a seagull. That's all I wanted to get straight...I'm not a seagull."

The red glow faded from Gubblebum's eyes; the snakes of electric charges hissed away but Gubblebum was still feeling cross.

"You look like a seagull, you talk...er...sound like a seagull...if you're not a seagull what on earth...I mean on sea are you?"

"Albert Ross at your service ladies," said the bird, doffing his old sailor's cap once more.
Gubblebum looked thoughtful. "If you're an albatross you'll know a lot about the sea...and the creatures that live in it."

"Arrr my hearties... I mean ladies...I've wandered the seven seas man and bird...I think I mean bird and bird. There's not a lot that Albert Ross doesn't know about the salty deep and what lives in it."

"So you'll know what's coming out of the salty deep you know so well and ruining the peace and beauty of my friend's home town...not to mention its hot-dog stalls?" said Gubblebum. The albatross lost its jaunty look for a second.

"Alas maties...I mean ladies...I haven't the foggiest idea what is causing this terrible damage to this lovely town. However, ship-mates...er...I mean ladies, I think I know someone who might be able to help you solve the mystery. What she doesn't know about what's going on down under isn't worth knowing,"

"She's Australian then, this friend of yours?" asked Amanda Salad.

"Australian? I don't quite...oh I see...down under...no ye swabs...I mean ladies...not that 'down under' - down under the sea. A princess...well a queen now she is...used to be the boss's daughter...until she met the prince that is."

"Where would we find this young lady?" asked Gubblebum.

"Talking to her only yesterday," said Albert, "Holding a reception on the Royal Yacht Lasagne for Royal Highness King Nick of Kleptomania...only a few miles from where we are standing...er... perching... er well I'm perching and you ladies are standing...er except for the beautiful baby of course who is lying,"

"This yacht is quite close, you say?" asked Gubblebum.

"That's right...just a few miles as the crow flies...well, as the albatross flies actually."

"And you could take us there?"

"Say the word," said the albratross, proudly puffing out the unruly feathers on his chest.

"I'll just go and get my broomstick," said Gubblebum. She turned to her friend. "Sorry Rolly - got carried away there...it's your town that is being wrecked. It's you who should find out if this Princess or Queen, whatever, can explain what is coming out of the sea every night rampaging around smashing up Baywitch and, more to the point - why? Besides, I can't go flying off on a sea-serpent hunt. Who'll look after the baby?"

Amanda Salad's eyes went all soft and dreamy. "I'd love to take care of him. You'd be as safe as castles with Auntie Salad Mandy-Pandy wouldn't oo iddums-diddums?" The baby gave a soft grunt and snorted; wriggled slightly and went on sleeping. Gubblebum looked across the sparkling waves...it would be a bit of an adventure and if she could find out who or what was causing the damage should be helping her dearest friend Amanda Salad.

"Well Rolly if you're sure it would be no trouble. Shouldn't take me a couple of shakes of a lamb's tail to nip over to the yacht; have a chat with the Princess and be back before he needs his next bottle or his nappy changed."

Amanda Salad gulped: she had not thought about some of the less iddum-diddums parts of baby care. "I'm sure it won't take you long and in any case I'll be able to cope," she said bravely, wondering if she'd be able to put the nappy on the baby at the right end.

"Right Rolly then that's settled. Albert, you stay here while I nip and fetch the old G.T.I. and off we go into the wild blue yonder."

Giving the baby a gentle kiss so as not to waken him and with a wave to Amanda Salad who was beginning to look distinctly worried as she thought what might be in store for her when iddums-diddums woke up, Gubblebum threw one red and yellow striped leg over her G.T.I. broomstick.

"Lead on Mac Ross....up, up and away... Geronimo!" With a high-powered snarl the broomstick soared into the sky following the albatross. What Gubblebum hadn't noticed was that Pancake had jumped aboard the broomstick and was digging his claws into the bristles trying to cling on whilst his long fur, ears and tail streamed out behind him.

After about half an hour's flying Albert slowed and pointed towards the crinkly blue sea with the tip of one wing. As he needed two wings to fly he nearly fell out of the sky and only saved himself after a couple of wild somersaults.

"She be down there Cap'n...er I mean your witchiness," panted Albert who had found flying in front of a G.T.I. broomstick something of an effort, "Not as young as I was...need to lose a bit of weight and cut down on the smoked herrings," he thought as he followed Gubblebum in a sweeping dive.

If you are thinking that the Royal Yacht Lasagne would be something like the boats you play with in the bath...you know, a pointy wooden bit and a little floppy sail like a hanky cut in half...you'd be wrong... very wrong. It was huge and white with hundreds of windows like lace holes in a shoe all along the side. What? A boat...er...ship doesn't have windows...okay, portholes!

If you were expecting billowing white sails, wrong again: there were two enormous funnels with the Royal Coat of Arms: some think that it looked like a loo brush with a whale and a lion playing pat-a-cake on either side of it.

On the pointy bit at the front which was slicing through the sparkling sea throwing up a big wave shaped a bit like Amanda Salad's mouth...only white of course...a big party was...what's that?...it's called the foredeck? Okay...on the foredeck a big party was in progress. Gentleman in embroidered velvet coats, coloured knee breeches, silken tights and silver buckled shoes danced with ladies with piled up hair and sticky out dresses which at times almost knocked over the side the waiters hurrying hither and yon with trays of food and drink.

As the elegant crowd heard the throaty burble as Gubblebum throttled back for a landing they all rushed to the side of the ship. It was a good job that it was such a big ship or their weight would have tipped it over and the sea would have been full of floating wigs and sticky out dresses. The Lord Chamberlain, a tubby little man whose pink silk tights, bulging pink coat, red face and curly white wig made him look like an angry strawberry ice cream with whipped cream on top, ran... well... *wobbled* to the ship's rail.

"Stern! Stern!" He yelled at Gubblebum, pointing towards the back of the boat which is called the stern. Gubblebum looked very stern when she heard the bossy little man giving her orders...he came very close to turning into a real strawberry ice cream...perhaps with a few baked beans and a slurp of gravy.

As Gubblebum flew over the blunt end of the boat... okay... 'stern'... she saw two circles painted on the floor...what?...oh, 'deck'. The first was white and had a large letter H in its centre while the second was black and had a large B. At first Gubblebum was a bit puzzled; then the penny dropped...good job it wasn't a real penny or it could have hit someone on the head.

"I get it," said Gubblebum, "H for helicopters and B for broomsticks...how convenient."

As softly as a drifting feather, Gubblebum set the G.T.I. broomstick right in the centre of the black circle. She turned to pick up her flight bag, forgetting that she hadn't brought one, and saw Pancake.

"Pancake! What on earth...well, what on sea are you doing here?"

Pancake was delighted to be on something solid even if it was bobbing up and down and rolling from side to side rather alarmingly. He rushed up to Gubblebum trying to jump up and lick her face. Unfortunately, the floor ...er... deck had just been washed... what?... oh, I see... the deck had been swabbed and was wet and slippery. Pancake didn't manage to lick Gubblebum's face but he did manage to knock her over sending her sliding on her red and yellow bottom like a deck-quoit right into the centre of the helicopter circle.

The witch sat in a soapy puddle thinking about dirty washing and ice cream and beans. Pancake leapt around her barking and wagging his tail, thinking this was a great game. He was so excited he nearly skidded over the side into the sea. Gubblebum's mind pictures of dozy dogs being turned into smelly or yucky things faded to be replaced by one of Pancake flying through the air and landing, splosh!, in the sea where there were sharks and other doggy-snacking creatures.

Gubblebum stood up, trying to pull her bright red miniskirt over the wet patch on her tights...after all she didn't want any of those posh people at the pointy-end party thinking she had...... well in any case, she didn't.

"Pancake stop racing around like a mad thing before you end up in a whale of a lot of trouble...or just in a whale. Calm down and let's go and see if we can find this Princess Thingy; ask if she knows what is battering Baywitch, then back before Rolly finds out that with babies there is a lot of stinkums-pinkums as well as iddums-diddums."

She started to walk towards the front... 'bow' of the ship, when the Lord Chamberlain wobbled towards her looking rather like strawberry jelly with whipped cream.

"I say...you there! Yes you - the common-person thingy with the smelly hind... You can't just land on Her Royal Highness Queen Coralia's yacht without so much as a by-or-leave and wearing those ghastly ordinary person clothes. I'm afraid I must ask you..." The strawberry Chamberlain noticed snakes of green light curling around the ends of the common person's fingers. Then he noticed he had begun to feel cold...very cold; several baked beans slithered down the front of his snowy wig and fell on his nose.

"What did you say?" asked Gubblebum in a calm voice which seemed to come from the depths of a freezer in an ice lolly factory near the North Pole.

"Er...er... I said I was afraid... and...er... I am...in fact, I'm terrified! What can I do your witchiness?"

The sight of the pompous little man turning into a real strawberry ice-cream with her special added topping made Gubblebum's tummy start to feel very funny, especially as the ship was lurching gently from side to side.

The green snaky lights disappeared and Lord Chamberlain began to feel warmer again though for several days afterwards he found cold baked beans in some of the strangest places...

"Tell Queen Coralia that Ms Gubblebum, BSc with Dishonours (it means British Sorcery Certificate) wishes to speak to her on a matter of some urgency," said Gubblebum, thinking that by this time it would be a matter of some urgency that the baby had a clean nappy.

"Certainly your witchship...I'll tell her at once...if not sooner," stammered the Lord Chamberlain and waddled off like a jet-propelled jelly, leaving a trail of baked beans on the newly-washed... oh wait, er...swabbed floor...er... deck.

Gubblebum arrived at the party and was greeted by five sweet little ladies in waiting. They all looked exactly the same. They wore spotless powdered wigs all exactly the same height and decorated with a large pink bow. They each wore a pink sticky out dress with no decoration except for a large pink rose. Their tights and shoes, all exactly the same, were also pink.

They all curtsied at exactly the same time and exactly the same amount; then, again at exactly the same time they held out their hands for Gubblebum to shake.

"Air Lair," they said in a chiming chorus, "Say nice to meet you. Lovely weath'ah we're heving, what? Sorry we don't know your name as we've never seen you arind any of our friends' hises or dine the tine."

"I'm afraid I don't get ite...I mean out much these days...what with the toffee-apples and helping Calvin with the balloon trips and the animals... then there's the baby - he takes up a lot of my time... but Rolly...I mean my friend Amanda Salad's taking care of him at the moment you see..."

Gubblebum realised that she was witcherring on and that the five prim little ladies did not have the faintest idea what she was talking abite...err...about. However, they all nodded politely exactly at the same time and murmured "High jolly interesting... Well must be orf and mingle, mingle, mingle... just one endless rind..." They moved away as if tied together and disappeared into the throng. The last Gubblebum heard of them was their tiny tinkling voices fading away, "Must mingle...mingle... mingle...mingle...min..."

"What well-mannered charming ladies... who were they?" Gubblebum asked the Lord Chamberlain who had at that moment come bustling towards her.

"Very well-bred young ladies to be sure, your witchiness. They are known throughout the land as the Nice Girls. Her Majesty will see you now if you will walk this way."

Gubblebum watched the Lord Chamberlain's bottom which reminded her of two elephants wrestling under an enormous silk blanket. "There's no way I would ever walk that way!" She muttered under her breath as she followed him towards the silver blue throne on which Queen Coralia was sitting. Suddenly from the top of the ship...oh, alright...the Bridge came a shout.

"Pirate ship on the starboard side! Prepare to repel boarders! Man the gun-decks ye swabs...eh...oh!" It was obvious that the lookout had just remembered...there were no guns or gun decks for that matter. They were at the mercy of the pirates!

There was panic. Gentleman ran hither and yon then turned round and ran yon and hither when they realised they were on a ship and there was only so far you could run without getting your feet very wet. They ran round in circles bumping into each other; knocking off wigs to reveal shiny bald heads. Ladies in sticky out dresses were brushed aside warbling like weebles trying not to fall over as they knew they would never regain their feet because of the sticky-outness of their dresses. One poor lady was knocked clean overboard where she bobbed in the waves like a blue silk buoy. A seagull was completely taken in and flew down to perch on her head.

Gubblebum, followed by Pancake, wriggled through the screaming lords and ladies and headed for the stairs to the Bridge. She saw the sinister black hull and blood red sails of the pirate vessel bearing down on the helpless Lasagne. Every inch of the rigging was packed with yelling ruffians in tattered clothes; red and white spotted bandannas around their heads; most had black eye patches and teeth to match. They waved their fearsome looking swords and huge pistols shouting rude piratical things like "Avast behind maties!" Which made the Nice Girls blush scarlet and the Lord Chamberlain looked decidedly uncomfortable.

Grappling hooks were thrown over the Lasagne's rails...one pirate lost four weeks pillaging money...he'd forgotten to tie a rope to his grappling hook and it went plop into the sea. The Buccaneers swarmed onto the Lasagne's scrubbed deck in their dirty bare feet. They were led by their captain; the most feared pirate on the seven seas...well, on five of them at least.

Battleship Grey Jake had learned his trade as a cabin boy under Blackbeard... Henry Morgan who was the most feared pirate on the seven seas...all seven of them. He was so horrible and cruel, that seven Seas was really not enough and he was feared on several large lakes as well!

Peter Flint

When he became the captain of the Bad Ship Chipaniola, Battleship Grey Jake had thought long and hard for a terrifying name: after all Clarence Clutterbimble was not a very scary name for a pirate. He had originally decided to call himself Black Jake but soon found that there were so many pirates with that name that there was no end of confusion and muddle. Like at the pirates' Christmas party all the places except one were labelled 'Black Jake' and no one knew where to sit. Fights broke out and Santa's sleigh took on an entirely different meaning. The other one? Oh, he'd called himself Lilac Jake: he was colour blind! The presents got completely mixed up. Black Jake, (the real one) had asked Santa for an especially sharp cutlass...with a soft plastic bit in the middle so it didn't hurt his teeth when he was boarding other ships. He got the Softee Sailors' Safety Hammock which came with specially low hooks for seafarers who were frightened of falling out of bed.

Clarence... I mean Battleship Grey Jake had tried to copy his old captain Henry Morgan by tying fireworks to his beard and lighting them. All that happened was that he set fire to his best hat with the ostrich plumes and the other pirates thought it was a party and lit a bonfire on the deck with disastrous results. Although there was nothing wrong with his eyes, he wore a black patch over the left one. To look extra tough he'd even tried wearing patches over both eyes but he kept bumping into things and several times fell overboard. He gave up this idea when he was chased by a large crocodile with a loud ticking noise coming from its stomach. His crew laughed themselves silly. They were fed up with fishing him out of the ocean and had made a large clockwork crocodile which they lowered into the sea each time Clarence toppled over the rail.

He had tried a wooden leg but keeping one leg bent up behind him looked awfully soppy and gave him the most terrible cramp. The hook didn't work either: when he thought no one was looking he'd started to pick his nose. The doctor said he'd make a full recovery and he'd even be able to smell properly...the other pirates thought this was wonderful as he'd smelt awful *before* the accident!

Finally he got a parrot which he called Captain Flinch...it was to have been Captain Flint but it kept pecking his ear. He got rid of it after a couple of weeks because its language was making the other pirates blush. Apart from swearing it could only say "Pieces of four" as it had only been half trained! Besides he had to keep sending his best velvet jacket...the one with the lacy cuffs...to the cleaners.

Things were going well for Battleship Grey Jake and his motley crew... (I wonder why crews are always motley?) The elegant ladies and gentlemen had been crowded right down into the sharp end of the ship. Some of the ladies were more worried about getting their beautiful sticky out dresses squashed than they were about being robbed or even poked with cutlasses.

A plank had been run out over the side and a couple of pirates who had studied at R.A.D.A (Ruffians and Desperadoes Acting) performed a vivid mime of what would happen to anyone who thought of hanging on to the odd diamond necklace, gold chain or jewelled medallion. Four evil looking rogues were going round collecting the sparklers in their three cornered hats... Jake had chosen these four not because of their villainous appearance but because they were the only ones who could afford hats... or perhaps they were the only ones with three cornered heads!

The hats were full to the brim with glittering treasure and Jake was looking around for something else to hold his booty...a boot perhaps...when he made his big mistake.

"Here you... yes you stripey stockings... run down to the kitchen, I mean the galley, and bring me a couple of the biggest saucepans you can find. Trot along now there's a good girl."

Gubblebum stood very still and took several deep breaths but little spits of green fire came from the ends of her fingers like those dud fireworks on Bonfire Night. It was bad enough calling her 'Stripy Stockings' when she'd put on her best red and yellow tights... £5.99 from M&S (Magicians and Sorcerors) but to call a witch 'a good girl' was about the worst insult anyone could think of. She took several more breaths and decided to do nothing: after all, losing a few gems would probably teach these pampered pointy-party-people a lesson.

Then Jake made a bigger mistake. "Arr, shiver me timbers yer lubbers," he growled...all pirates say stupid things like this when they are trying to act tough. "Here's a wench what thinks her's a match for Battleship Grey Jake me hearties." All pirates also stop speaking grammatically as soon as they've taken the pirate oath. "We'll see who's the Cap'n on this flea-ridden tub... arr or me name 'aint Battleship Grey Jake...bring that mangy dog over here...arr!"

Several pirates started grabbing anyone close to them even some of their own comrades as calling someone a 'mangy dog' was almost as commonplace as bursting into a chorus of "Yo Ho Ho and a bottle of rum" on the slightest excuse.

"No! No! Ye scurvy lubbers...the real mangy dog...her'll do as she'm told when she sees the mutt walk the plank and drop into Davy Jones' Locker."

Pancake, who hadn't met many pirates, didn't know that Davy Jones' Locker was the seamen's name for the bottom of the ocean so he wagged his tail when one of the pirates grabbed his collar. He trotted eagerly towards the plank thinking that Mr Jones had his locker in a strange place but perhaps he had some doggie-chocs in it...who could tell with humans!

Perhaps it was the eye-patch but anyone who described the Royal Yacht Lasagne as a flea-ridden tub might be excused for not noticing that the feeble little sparks on the ends of Gubblebum's fingers were now jets of flame like welding torches. Worse still, they had turned a deep purple. Jake was just about to utter another mouthful of pirate gobble-dee-gook when he did notice that the purple flames were pointing at him! Jake's mouth fell open.

There was a tremendous roaring sound like a school-full of children at going home time; the purple flames grew and grew, hissing and boiling until ten misty dragon-creatures with flaring nostrils and curving talons towered over the deck. Gubblebum shook her hands as if shaking off drops of water and the ten demons fell from the sky onto the cringing pirates. Jake's mouth closed.

To the astonishment of all the ladies and gentlemen, the pirate holding Pancake's collar walked jerkily backwards to where he had grabbed him...and let go. Jake began shouting something in what sounded like a foreign language but which they later realised was back-to-front pirate gibberish. The two R.A.D.A. pirates went through their mime...in reverse. The four gew-gaw collectors walked around backwards taking jewellery from their hats and giving it back. The entire pirate crew scrambled backwards over the rail onto the deck of their own vessel. The grappling-hooks magically unhooked themselves and flew back into the hands of the pirates who looked puzzled...all except the one who'd forgotten to tie a rope to his hook. When it flew up out of the sea into his hand he grinned as he realised he'd not lose his hook or his pillaging-money.

The whole pirate crew then climbed backwards onto the rails and rigging of their ship and began grinning and shouting rude-sounding things in the same foreign language Jake had used. They were still shouting as the Chipaniola sailed backwards into the distance until it became a dot on the horizon before disappearing altogether. Gubblebum rubbed her hands to get rid of a few glowing purple embers.

"That's the way to deal with video pirates," she grinned. Gubblebum

turned to see Queen Coralia beckoning
her. Coralia was strikingly beautiful
although her skin was a dead white
with a faint bluish tinge and her hair,
long and auburn, had a greenish hue
and curious lumpy bits which she
insisted were curls. She gave off a
faint fishy smell which she tried in
vain to cover up by wearing lots of
perfume... unfortunately, her favourite
was 'Poisson'.

"You'd never guess that she was
once a barmaid," whispered a be-
wigged gentleman to Gubblebum as she
approached the Queen.

"Mermaid! She was a mermaid, you
fool!" hissed his companion. As
Gubblebum neared the queen a
gentleman, his wig sadly askew and
voice slurred from too many visits to
the silver dolphin-shaped champagne
fountain, grabbed her arm and said. "I

shay...just been to the loo...(he actually meant the heads)...old thing... drefffull racket going on up here, what... have... have... I mished something?"

Gubblebum smiled. "Well there was a load of pirates but they've all gone."

The gentleman gulped. "I've eaten some funny things at this party...boar's head, turtle eggs, larks' tongue, chocolate-coated ants, wiggedy grubs but I've never had a rat in a pie. Shtill, if they've all gone as you shay young fella me lad it doeshn't look as if I'll get the chance." He staggered away towards the dolphin fountain muttering, "Pie rats, pie-rats whatever will they think of next?"

Coralia smiled and held out her hand. "Thank you, thank you for getting rid of those horrid pirates... ouch...

ouch... sorry...er...your witchiness...I must sit down...my feet are killing me... all the dancing you know," she flopped gracefully onto the silver blue throne and waved for a servant to bring a golden chair for Gubblebum. "Can I get you something to drink? To eat? How about a nice plate of wiggedy grubs followed by a bowl of chocolate-coated ants?"

Gubblebum tried not to let Coralia see her shudder. "I would like a drink: creating those fire-dragons is quite a dry spell." Coralia sent a servant scurrying off to the fountain. She patted Gubblebum's hand saying, "To what do we owe the pleasure of your visit...er...er?"

Gubblebum knew that to err is human so she decided not to be offended. "My name is Gubblebum your Highness and I need your help."

"Anything, anything Gubblebum sweetie... I knew you hadn't just dropped in on the off chance... when I say 'dropped in' I don't mean you actually dropped in: you landed like a feather... best broomstick flying I've seen in a long time. Well Gubby, darling your wish is my command as they say...'they' usually say it: you see darling, normally it's the other way round for me... like my wish is their command if you catch my drift."

"I just wanted to ask..."

"Just name it Gubbykins...as long as it's not too complicated...those dreadful pirates have given me the most awful headache and the Lord

Chamberlain tells me there's no pain-killers left on the whole ship...not one!"

"No pain-killers... why is that?"

Coralia punched Gubblebum on the shoulder and gave a loud horsey laugh - or perhaps it was more like a sea horsey laugh.

"Because the pirates ate 'em all...get it Gubby-pie? The pirates ate 'em all!" She laughed so loud, rocking from side to side in her merriment that Gubblebum thought the throne would topple over. Wiping her eyes, Coralia apologised and again asked Gubblebum how she could reward her for saving her ship and her friends from Battleship Grey Jake and his band of cutthroats. As briefly as she could before the queen could think of any more awful jokes Gubblebum explained about her visit to Amanda Salad and how her friend's home town was being smashed up by invisible sea-serpents.

"Father!" exclaimed Coralia.

Gubblebum was puzzled. "Your father's a sea-serpent?"

"No, Gubblypoos silly...daddy's the King of the ocean...King Raptune."

"Er, don't you mean...er Neptune?"

"He was until I bought him that Sea-Dee player for Christmas...now it's Rap, Rap from low-tide to high...blame myself...should never have used wrapping-paper to parcel it up."

"And you think he'll be able to help me find these sea-serpents?"

"Sure of it sweetie... come with me... walk this way." Gubblebum followed the queen down to her magnificent bedroom... er... cabin. On the walls beautiful animals of the forest and mountains ran through golden hills and meadows while the ceiling was a deep blue, almost black where glittering sea-creatures leapt and glided through silver reefs.

"Let me introduce you to the only friend daddy would allow me to bring to your human world." Coralia pressed a button; a curtain slid back to reveal an enormous fish-tank. It was so large that Gubblebum wondered if it was, in fact, a glass panel looking out into the depths of the ocean. A huge shiny blue and green lobster scuttled up to the glass waving its claws excitedly.

"Thermidor I would like you to meet my new friend, Gubblebum."

The lobster folded his claws across his carapace; bowed and said in a refined if somewhat bubbly voice, "A pleasure to make your acquaintance ma'am."

"Thermidor, I have a special job for you...do it right and I'll see you get the starring role at the palace Christmas Party."

"And what might that be, Your Majesty?" sighed the lobster.

"Santa Claws!" screeched Coralia. The lobster sighed again...

"Three thousand, six hundred and fifty-seven," he thought wearily. "The special mission Your Majesty?" he said before Coralia could do the ones about 'prawn-shops' or 'feeling crabby'.

"Piece of fish-cake, Thermy old thing... just escort Gubbibobbles here to Daddy's palace...prawn-toe."

"Missed that one," thought Thermidor. "At once Majesty...in fact the sooner the better," he said, though the last part was under his breath...I suppose 'under his absorption of oxygen through his gills' would be more accurate but you must admit it is a bit long-winded and, after all, it's only a story anyway.

Gubblebum was getting worried about the baby...and even more worried about Amanda Salad so she was anxious to be off. Suddenly she realised that this posed a considerable problem. Thermidor could absorb oxygen but neither she nor Pancake could breathe under water. A spell would have solved the difficulty in no time but routing the pirates had run her magic pretty low.

Suddenly she had an idea... Gubble-dee-goo! She felt in her pocket and as luck would have it...OK, I'll admit it...I made sure she had some or we couldn't get on with the story, could we? She found a large dollop wrapped in a recipe for Witches on Broomsticks.

"Thank you Coralia...you've been a great help. Lead the way Thermidor. Pancake, heel!"

Pancake looked puzzled as Calvin and Gubblebum had long ago despaired of getting him to sit; walk on; beg; play dead or any of the other tricks soppy dogs would do to get a biscuit. The only

command he knew was "Eat"! I suppose
if they'd said "Chase Rabbits!" he would
have played ball...I mean...he would
have done as he was told but this
order seemed hardly necessary. He
assumed that his mistress was just
showing off using nautical terms. As he
was on a ship, he followed her leaning
to one side.

When they reached the deck
Thermidor wriggled over the side and
plumped into the water. Gubblebum put
the wodge of delicious Gubble-dee-goo
in her mouth and began to chew. Then
she puffed out her cheeks and blew
surrounding herself and Pancake with
a large bubble which she rolled off the
ship into the sea where Thermidor was
waiting. Poking a hole in the bubble
she released a jet of air which sent it
scooting along the sea-bed after the
lobster.

"Brilliant," thought Gubblebum, "I suppose I should call it Subble-Dee-Goo now."

Through fantastic forests of gently waving sea-plants, past towering reefs like castle walls built from pink sugar-icing they made their way along the ocean floor. Several times they saw the sad wooden skeletons of ships muffled in weed and barnacles. One of these seemed to be shivering and Gubblebum thought some powerful current must run through this part of the depths. As they approached, the vessel trembled more violently and Gubblebum was astonished to hear a voice saying, "Keep away! Don't touch me...I can't cope with visitors...you should have rung first...I've nothing to offer you...Oh dear...Oh dear...Whatever am I going to do?"

"Take no notice of her," said Thermidor, "She's just a nervous wreck." They swept past reefs and grottos. Gubblebum was delighted by the vivid colours of the fish which darted like living jewels around the Subble-Dee-Goo.

"Nearly there!" shouted Thermidor. Just as he did so, four large fish swam right up to the bubble. They were round and gleaming, they had huge fan-shaped tails which waved sinuously to and fro as they peered into the Subble-Dee- Goo. Each was a different colour: red, yellow, and green; while the largest of the four was a bright purple. All had pale shimmering patches on their bulging bellies.

"Welcome to the Kingdom of King Raptune. We have been sent to meet you. My name is Bob. Allow me to introduce my companions. This is Bob and over there is Bob and, last but not least, Bob. We are advisors to King Raptune. We call ourselves..."

"Let me guess," said Gubblebum, "the Advice Girls!"

The fish looked at each other in total bewilderment. "You must excuse us dear lady but we do not understand. We are the Tailly Guppies...perhaps you've heard of us?"

"I am sorry but I haven't... first time Pancake and I have sunk to the depths... I mean been in this neck of the woods... er this side of the bed...er...sea-bed."

"We understand dear lady. Do not distress yourself. If you would just follow us we'll be there in two shakes of a flounder's fin."

The Palace of King Raptune was too marvellous to describe...oh alright I'll try but don't blame me if it doesn't sound as marvellous as you expect! A long avenue flanked by enormous golden statues of the most exotic sea creatures led to a broad courtyard. The floor of this great circle was paved with millions of tiny rubies and emeralds. In the centre stood a gigantic throne carved from dazzling white coral and covered with a canopy lined with shells which glowed and shimmered in a thousand rainbow colours. There were, of course, many other parts of this splendid palace but they don't feature in this story so if you want to see them you'll have to use your own imagination!

When Gubblebum, Pancake, Thermidor and the Bobs arrived before the gleaming white throne, the whole place seemed deserted. As if from nowhere a dozen dolphins, wearing baseball caps back to front appeared at the side of the throne and began to sway and chant:

"Take up positions of prostration,
As you meet the leader of this nation.
He has wisdom: he has power,
Strong and tall as any tower.
We want you to accept the notion,
He's the main man in the ocean,
Raptune, Raptune long may he rule,
'Cos he is hip and he is cool."

"When he was King Neptune they used to blow conch shells," said Thermidor sadly.

A troupe of mermen all with bulging biceps, powerful pectorals, jutting jaws and terrific tails swam down the avenue and spread out on either side of the great throne. They raised golden tridents in the air... well, the water...

and shouted with one voice. "Long live King Raptune!"

The King took his place attended by two gorgeous mermaids who looked so much like Coralia that they had to be her sisters. Gubblebum hoped that their jokes would be better especially as there were two of them. Thermidor went forward, bowed to the King then to the two princesses. "With your Majesty's gracious permission, I present Her Witchiness the Lady Gubblebum."

Gubblebum bowed and Pancake wagged his tail and jumped up and down sending the Subble-Dee-Goo shooting forward to knock down half the mermen like a row of skittles. As they were under the sea the water cushioned their fall and none of them was hurt.

The King thought it was very funny and laughed and laughed, sending his long white beard streaming out like a billowing flag.

"Must be dashed uncomfortable in that bubble-thingy me dear. Never mind, soon put that right." He waved his jewelled trident above his head and muttered deep into his beard. There was a roar like surf breaking on a rocky beach and the Subble-Dee-Goo disappeared.

Gubblebum held her breath - her face turning a deep red. Again the King roared with laughter.

"You needn't do that me dear...let go or you'll burst. You'll find you'll be able to breathe just like you earthlings do... up there!" the King shuddered, "If you don't believe me look at your dog-fish thingy...and don't worry about your subblemarine I'll see you get it back in tip-top condition when you leave."

Gubblebum looked where the King pointed to see Pancake leaping up to one of the dolphins trying to lick its face... well its front-end. She let out her breath in a great gasp which sent a fountain of bubbles spiralling upwards.

"Come here Pancake you naughty dog...you're doing that on porpoise!" The two Coralia lookalike princesses groaned.

The King called one of the mermen who swam away and came back a moment or two later with a giant turtle on a lead. The turtle swam lazily to the foot of the throne then lay down tucking in its legs and after cocking a wary glance at Pancake, pulling in its huge scaly head.

"Sit down me dear." boomed Raptune, indicating the turtle shell.

At first Gubblebum was afraid that she might hurt the poor creature but the King laughed and said, "Don't worry about Michelle... no dearie... not my shell, I don't have a shell as you can see... Michelle...it's her name...the turtle. We were going to call her Myrtle but Myrtle Turtle is a bit much...don't you think?" Still not wishing to damage Michelle, Gubblebum sat rather gingerly on her back.

"Thermidor tells me you saved me daughter from some pirates and that you are having a spot of bother with sea-serpents. Can be a right nuisance at times..."

Gubblebum was not sure whether Raptune was talking about pirates or sea-serpents or, perhaps, both for his voice tailed away. He gave a deep sigh. "She was the most headstrong of the three of them... never gave me a minutes peace but I still do miss her you know... Coralia. Wonderful sense of humour... never stopped telling jokes."

He sighed again shaking three large goldfish out of his beard.

"Don't you ever see her?" asked Gubblebum gently.

"Tried it once me dear... never again... land-sick the whole time... damned place never stopped standing still... and that husband of hers..."

"Not exactly what you wanted for her..."

The King groaned, "When I think of all the Mer-Princes she could have had. Like piranha around a lobster pot they were...tripping over Princes all over the palace I was... The Count of Finland, the Duck of Clambodia, the Potentate of Poolland, the Nabob of New Sealand and the Prince of Whales and she picked him..."

"Who, your Majesty?" whispered Gubblebum, intrigued despite herself.

"Him... King Squiffy of Dipsomania... Poseidon help us! Never forget that visit..."

"He didn't make you welcome?"

"That's just it lass - he did... too welcome... I should have guessed shouldn't I? From the name of his

Kingdom... I should have Known better... never again... no, never again..."

"I'm sorry, your Highness but you've lost me..."

"He drinks me dear...like a fish...well, more like a human actually...fountains in every room of his castle...even the loos...wine, wine, champagne...you name it. I should've Known better... Kept offering you see... not polite to refuse... he wouldn't take no for an answer..."

"And you got..."

"Legless...me dear...ashamed to admit it but it's true...totally legless."

He shook his head as if to chase away the memory, "Sorry, mustn't bore you with my problems...you said something about sea-serpents?"

Gubblebum told her story and was surprised when, without any comment, King Raptune clapped his hands and said in a regal tone, "Bring the Great Pearl!"

Two of the mermen swam off and returned carrying a huge pink shell which twinkled with points of blue light. The mermen placed the shell reverently on an exquisite coral table. All the other mermen raised their tridents and shouted,

"Behold the Great Pearl of Wisdom!" As the shouts died away, the shell slowly opened to reveal a flawless black pearl about the size of a football. King Raptune went to the pearl and placed one hand on its smooth surface. Immediately there boiled inside the ebony ball, wreaths of red and purple smoke. For a few moments the clouds of smoke seethed and curled then vanished.

Inside the globe was a picture of a world of ice as far as the eye could see: mountains and valleys of blinding white under a sky of quivering blue. Slowly the picture changed. Cracks formed on the shimmering blankness through which dark channels of violet water could be seen. These channels broadened; whole cliffs of bluish ice broke and fell into the white-capped waves. Again the picture changed. Now there were barren rocks lapped by the rising sea. Higher and higher it rose until it steadied and the water rose no further. Now the pearl showed a valley between high mountains. Although the sea was no longer rising, water was welling up from the valley floor as if some vast underground tunnel connected with the ocean beyond the mountains.

King Raptune sat forward on his throne gazing rapt at the unfolding story, "I remember this," he said, "many thousands of years ago when I was a young mermen the ice melted from the land and the ocean rose but there was a passageway through which the water flooded back. It had to be blocked. I undertook the task... see!"

Now the picture showed the King - young and strong, his flowing hair and beard black as night. Carrying some huge object in his mighty arms he was twisting and turning in a maelstrom of rushing pounding water. His back straining, he braced himself against the awesome power of the current and released his burden. Magically the sea around him calmed.

Once more the globe went dark. The King beckoned to the two mermen who moved forward to remove the Pearl of Wisdom but the pearl had not given up all its secrets. The darkness was the depths of rushing water inside the tunnel under the earth now blocked at the seaward end. Suddenly there was a blinding light as the last of the water drained into the Valley Lake taking with it an enormous green snakelike creature...a sea serpent!

Suddenly there was not one sea serpent but four! At first the watchers thought that the pearl was suffering interference but on closer inspection they saw that the enormous creatures were different colours. There was a red one, a blue one, a sort of mauve and red stripy one and a bright yellow one

93

with large pink spots. For a while they swam aimlessly, twisting and turning around each other like party streamers. The pearl went black.

"What a marvellous thing," said Gubblebum, thinking such an object could perk up her own witchcraft no end, "I expect you had to journey to the far corners of your ocean realm and snatch the pearl from the lair of a ferocious sea dragon?"

"£14:95 from Amazon... bought on-line... fishing line of course! There's your answer me dear... it's clear as saltwater."

It wasn't at all clear to Gubblebum. "I'm sorry Your Majesty," she said, "but..."

"You saw it me dear. When I bunged up that hole to stop the sea flooding back onto the land those unfortunate creatures must have been swimming past. One of them...the green one was...er...well there's no other way to describe it...er...flushed down the pipe."

"Very unfortunate but what does it have to do with my friend Amanda Salad and Baywitch being wrecked every night?"

"It's the legend me dear..." said the King.

"Legend?"

"An old mer-legend which says that the lost one shall be found when the witch forsakes the land for the depths of the sea. Somehow those four poor creatures must have found out... don't ask me how... that your friend...what was her name again me dear?"

"Amanda Salad...er...she's a sandwitch you see."

"That's the one...forget me own name next... memory like a sieve...not that one of those would be a lot of use down here...eh, what?"

"About the sea-serpents and the legend, your Majesty?"

"Oh yes...where was I? Well, according to the legend, the Four Serpents of the Apuckerlips have been searching for their lost sister for thousands of years and she will only be found when the witch forsakes the land for the sea. They must have thought...your friend... what was her name? Don't tell me...I've got it...Amanda Salad was the witch mentioned in the legend. Gone looking for her, my dear. Searching for thousands of years...must have been at their witch's...I mean wits end, don't you know. Mind you it's a bit tricky working out which end the sea serpent keeps its wits... much the same at both ends...what?"

Gubblebum wasn't sure whether Raptune wanted a reply but before she could think of one the Pearl of Wisdom began to pulse with a terrifying red and orange glow turning a deep sinister purple tinged with streaks of black. The King and all his court seemed to shrink back in fear and with one voice they murmured, "Leviathan!"

When they dared to look again at the pearl it was once more a smooth glossy sphere of impenetrable blackness. Gubblebum just had to ask.

"Er... this er... Leviathan your Majesty... well... er... I couldn't help noticing you all seemed a teensy bit worried."

The King shuddered, "Leviathan is...well, let me put it this way...think of your very worst nightmare...falling into a barrel full of snakes...a spider in the bath three feet across and using all the hot water...a teacher with extra long fingernails scraping them sl-o-o-o-wly down the blackboard...a bowl of strawberry ice cream with baked beans and gravy... whatever... multiply that by ten and you'll still be a long way from how awful Leviathan is."

"But what is this Leviathan?" asked Gubblebum thinking of that horrid Brian who'd put a worm down her back when she was little...ugh!

"He...she...it...is a monster me dear...so evil and powerful that even I'm afraid of it...well, a bit."

"What does this terrible monster look like?"

"Huge and dark and unbelievably cruel. I can't tell you much more than that me dear as no one who has strayed into Leviathan's territory has ever come back...ever!"

"But...if we keep well out of its way..."

"You saw the pearl me dear. If you want to help your friend, somehow we've got to get the five sea-serpents back together."

"Yes I can see that but how do we do it?"

"We've got to open up that tunnel again so that the sea serpent in the lake can swim through to join the others in the sea," said Raptune.

"But your Majesty, even with all your strength you could hardly hold out against the force of the water. Besides, how will the trapped sea serpent know that the tunnel is open again?" She tactfully didn't mention that the King was older now.

"I never said it would be easy-peasy but I have a plan. It was many thousands of years ago that I blocked the tunnel and the levels of the seas and the waters of the land have settled down. Perhaps the pressure will not be so great as it was when the ice was melting...we can only hope."

"How can we warn the sea-serpent to be ready... when...if we are able to re-open the passageway to the sea?" said Gubblebum, half to the King and half thinking aloud. "I think I have an idea. Can you get a message to your daughter Coralia, your Majesty?"

"Of course: I can send old Thermidor with a message...be there in two wags of a lobster's tail. What do you want me to tell me little girl?"

"Tell her to get Albert Ross to fly to the lake with a message saying that we are going to try to clear the tunnel first thing tomorrow...or whatever it is under the sea."

"Sorry me dear but how do you know the blasted bird will still be around young Coralia's little boat-thingy?"

"There was enough food left at the pointy-party to feed all the albatrosses in existence and of all of the albatrosses in existence I'm fairly confident Albert will be the last to run out...I mean...fly out... on a free lunch."

"Right lassie, that's settled: I'll give Thermidor his swimming orders; gather me brave merlads for a briefing; pop you and your dog-fish thingy back into your balloon-thingy then off we go to organise the sea-serpents get-together...and you don't see many of them in a short swim I can tell you."

"I hate to be a wet week or even a wet witch but what if we can't move whatever you use to block the tunnel, your Majesty?"

"Think positive me dear. Remember the poem..." Rapture cleared his throat, placed one hand on his chest, held the Trident high in the other and declaimed in a very stagey voice:

"They said that the job just couldn't be done,
But he smiled and buckled down to it,
He tackled the job that couldn't be done..."

Gubblebum finished the verse, "And couldn't do it!"

Rapture turned bright red and mumbled, "Must have been thinking of some other blasted poem...er would it be that one about a lad on a burning deck? Anyway, you get the general idea."

"I hate to carp on keeping, your Highness... I mean keep on keeping carp...no... I hate to keep on carping but haven't we forgotten Leviathan? The pearl seemed to show that it was prowling the ocean floor near the tunnel."

The King shuddered. "We'll just have to pray that it's gone for a nap while we're busy... I'd keep a few spells up your sleeve me dear just in case."

Thermidor was dispatched to swim...or scuttle... I'm not really sure about lobster propulsion... back to the yacht. King Raptune assembled all his toughest mermen and made a rousing speech during which he began the poem about the impossible task...stuttered a bit before finishing with something about a boy on a burning ship. The mermen looked puzzled.

At last all was ready and Raptune raised his Trident: muttered into his beard and Gubblebum and Pancake were once again inside their Subblemarine.

The journey to the blocked tunnel did not take long. It would have taken even less time if Raptune hadn't got lost a couple of times. Still it had been thousands of years since he'd been to that part of the ocean. I suppose this story would have been more exciting if they had adventures like travelling through seaweed forests in which lurks giant squid... should that be squids? Or crossed enormous caverns with glowing pits of lava and roaring geysers of fire but I have to save one or two ideas for other stories...don't I?

"If memory sieves me right...I mean serves me right it was somewhere around here," said Raptune, "Clear away some of that seaweed me merry merlads."

The mermen set to work with a will forking to one side huge bundles of weed. Suddenly one shouted excitedly, "Your Majesty! Your Witchiness! I think I've found something."

They hurried over to where he stood... (floated?)... and sure enough at the foot of a rocky outcrop there it was. Gubblebum wasn't at all certain what she had expected to see but whatever it was it was not what she actually saw. At first she couldn't believe her eyes but it was true: the passage to the lake was stopped with an ordinary everyday bath plug! Admittedly it was a rather large bath plug but a bath plug it was: whitish rubber with a chain and everything.

"Right lads," called Raptune, grabbing hold of the chain, "all hands to the pumps...er...the chain."

All the muscular mermen took hold of the chain and Raptune ordered them to heave. I suppose had it been on land sweat would have been pouring from their knotted arms, bulging chests and even from their threshing tales. Under the sea nothing of the sort happened but it was evident from the agonised expressions on their contorted faces that they were straining every nerve and sinew. Once the plug moved and was lifted out of its hole, it then slapped back again with sucking noise.

Gubblebum could see that mere...or mer...muscle-power was not going to succeed. She closed her eyes and began to mutter under her breath. The first sign that anything was happening inside the bubble was that Pancake's fur began to glow bright green and stand stiffly on end. Although he looked like a large untidy glowing dandelion-clock, Pancake didn't appear to be the slightest bit concerned. I expect having lived all those years with Gubblebum he'd become used to all manner of strange occurrences.

Gubblebum's muttering became louder and her eyes scrunched up so tightly that her face looked like a screwed up paper hankie. The bubble filled with an eerie emerald light, then from its front, two shining green ropes as thick as a man's leg shot out and gripped the chain. As Rapture and the mermen strained, these glowing ropes shortened. Slowly the giant bath plug began to move out of its seating: a gurgle of water surged around its edge. The plug moved a little more as the magic ropes tightened and the King and his followers pulled until their eyes bulged.

Gubblebum, still muttering an incantation which was so rapid that it sounded like static on a badly tuned radio, opened her eyes to see that the plug was almost free. She was about to relax her concentration when the sea darkened as if covered by a purple cloak. Gubblebum looked up through the Gubble-Dee-Goo at the giant shadow which loomed menacingly over the little group.

"Cloaks and cauldrons - its Leviathan!" muttered Gubblebum, her concentration slipped and the taut, green ropes faded then disappeared in a shower of tiny emerald stars.

The King and his mermen were so caught up in their task that they were totally unaware of the danger which hovered above them. However, when Gubblebum's magic ropes dissolved they found the effort of pulling a huge plug impossible without them. Still clinging to the chain, King and mermen were dragged forward as the plug sloshed back into the hole. As they looked around to see why, on the point of success Gubblebum had abandoned them, they saw the rippling purple horror which stretched endlessly above them. Grabbing their tridents they formed a protective circle around their King.

They might as well have been holding straws for the purple cloud swayed and billowed and the mermen were swept away like so many grains of sand. Only the King remained, alone, his jewelled Trident held ready to do battle with the terrifying monster. Giving his battle cry: "For cod and fishtory!" He sprang forward only to be met by a blinding jet of ink squirted from somewhere amid the rising purple folds. The ink spray sent the King tumbling, choking, gasping far along the sandy bed of the ocean.

Gubblebum was alone...well Pancake was with her but rabbits were more his cup of tea... if he had drunk tea that is... than a sea monster which went on forever. Gubblebum gulped and raised her arms as the undulating purple cloud seemed to gather itself to destroy them. Only a few splurges of green fire dribbled from her finger-ends as the strain of trying to move the mammoth bath plug had, once again, drained her magic-battery almost flat. She gulped again.

The sea went dark as the creature swooped down for the kill. Gubblebum saw gleaming skin, purple darkening to black, in the folds of which loathsome scaly creatures all eyes and claws squirmed and scuttled. Then there was the fearsome red horror of its mouth like looking into a drooling volcano with teeth. Now Pancake whined, shrank back as far as the Gubble-Dee-Goo would stretch. Gubblebum closed her eyes and a tear trickled down her cheek as she thought she'd never see Calvin or the baby again.

Out of the whirling storm of weed and sand set up by Leviathan's passage through the water, an enormous whipping tentacle covered in slimy-grey-green suckers curled around the bubble containing the witch and her trembling pet. Slowly, as if playing with them like a cat with a mouse, the tentacle tightened. Even the magic Gubble-Dee-Goo could not resist this relentless pressure and stretched and stretched until it resembled one of those old-fashioned things grannies used to have to time eggs boiling. Pancake was in one end of the 'egg timer' while Gubblebum was in the other and the middle was being squeezed thinner and thinner until it snapped with a loud 'Twang'!

The volcano mouth opened and loomed over the semi-bubble containing Gubblebum. Now Pancake was not very bright but he was very brave and when he saw Leviathan about to gobble up his mistress he became very angry. He realised that this creature was bigger than a rabbit... a bit... but he reckoned a few sharp nips on its rear end would soon send it packing. Barking and snarling, he leapt forward. He had, of course, forgotten something... well, I told you he wasn't very bright. Have you spotted it? That's right... he was still in his half of the bubble!

As he made his gallop forward, the leaping and scrabbling sent the bubble shooting erratically in all directions. Leviathan's attention was diverted from his tasty witchy-snack by this curious tiny noisy creature which was bobbing up and down in his wrapping like a ping-pong ball at a shooting gallery. Another slithery tentacle reached out to catch this annoying morsel which wouldn't be polite enough to stay still to be eaten.

As the tentacle flailed around trying to grasp Pancake's bubble, it became entangled with the chain on the giant bath plug. Leviathan lashed frantically to free itself... out plopped... the bath plug and out shot a green body which didn't blot out as much sunlight as Leviathan but which was easily as long. The sea serpent was free!

Immediately the sea serpent attacked the monster, wrapping its coils around the slithery purple bulk and slashing with rows of great razor sharp teeth. The sea boiled and turned a milky white in which the battle of the two sea creatures looked like a grotesque shadow-play.

Gubblebum felt her bubble rising until it shot out into the sunlight. A moment later her heart leapt with joy as out of the waves came Pancake still leaping and barking furiously inside his half of the bubble.

Even now they were not safe as the titanic contest created towering waves which threatened to squash the bubbles and their occupants flat as pancakes... well as flat as one Pancake and one witch! Eventually the wave subsided and the surface of the sea was as smooth as a baby's b... er... as smooth as a millpond. Gubblebum had now recharged enough to manoeuvre her half of the bubble alongside Pancake. He was so delighted to see her safe and sound that he began leaping and scrabbling, again sending his half of the bubble bouncing and skipping over the surface like a skimming stone. Gubblebum sighed and used a little more of her precious magic to catch up to him again.

Far off in the distance...well it would be in the distance if it was far off, wouldn't it? What's that? Get on with the story...ooh bossy! Okay, a long way away, Gubblebum could see a pretty little seaside town. "Why its Baywitch. I'd recognise it anywhere." Convenient eh? That they should happen to bob up right opposite Baywitch beach? Okay, okay I know...get on with the story. Where was I? Oh yes...

"I'd recognise it anywhere... but I don't remember all those bridges. I've often seen a pair of bridges when I'm washing Calvin's kit for a children's party or he's off doing princey-things... oh, that's britches... anyway, britches or bridges, I've never seen eight of them in a line and all... er...all green... eh oh!" thought Gubblebum as the two semi-bubbles got nearer the shore.

Suddenly their fragile craft was tossed violently hither and yon and would almost certainly have capsized except that it is impossible to capsize the bubble... because its round you see. Out of the sea right in front of them reared an enormous snakelike head. A cavernous mouth opened to reveal row upon row of nasty looking dentistry. Slowly the great head...complete with teeth... lowered towards them.

"Out of the Leviathan into the fire," thought Gubblebum.

"So sorry I couldn'a stop for a chat when we last met Gubblebum ma wee lassie," said the sea-serpent, "I could see you were having a wee spot of bother with that there Leviathan...nae good'll come of that yin still I expect his mither loves him. Och hark at me blathering on...well when you've not spoken to a single body for thousands of years yer fair dying for a wee chat...catch up on all the latest gossip and such like. Och a'm off again and ye'll have nae idea who ah am."

Gubblebum couldn't help thinking that you didn't bump into green sea-serpents as long as a fair-sized river everyday while shopping in the supermarket so she had a suspicion of who this amiable creature might be.

"I'm awfully sorry but I don't think I caught your name..." she said.

"Och that's because ah didnae throw it lassie," laughed the sea-serpent, causing the two bubbles to dip and bob alarmingly, "Ma name's Playful-Ness but ye ken a've been locked up in that lake for so long now that everybody calls me...Loch-Ness."

"But how did you come to know my name?" asked Gubblebum.

"Well lassie, after ah'd sent that nae-guid Leviathan hame wi'a flea in his ear...so to speak, ah had a long chat with King Raptune. Och, he's alright... a wee bit ink-stained but nothing a bar of green soap and a hard scrubbing brush can't cure. He told me how ye were trying to set me free from that lake and stop ma four sisters smashing up yer friend's hame-town. He told me what a brave wee lassie ye were. Ah'm verra grateful and if there's ever anything ah can do tae repay ye... well ye've only got tae ask..."

"Well if you could have a wee...I mean a little word with your sisters I'd be very pleased and I'm sure my friend Amanda Salad would be too."

"Consider it done, lassie. Och ah cannae wait tae see their wee smiling faces again...a right bunch of scallywags we were... before the ice covered everything. There was Haughty-Ness... she was the eldest... thought she was the cat's pyjamas she did. Then there was the red one... Ruddiness... very shy she was... blushed scarlet every time anyone looked at her... though with her colour naebody noticed. Next came Spooky-Ness... loved practical jokes she did... she used to pop up alongside the beach when it was packed wi folk on holiday. She almost got a starring part in a film once but they gave it to some wee shark. Last but not least was ma wee baby sister, Cuddly-Ness...ah cannae wait tae hold her in ma coils again. Just think, lassie the times we could have had if it hadnae been fer that ice..."

"I suppose...when you were all together, that is, people called you the Ice Girls," said Gubblebum.

"Nay, Gubblebum, dearie why would onybody be sae daft as to call us that?"

"Just a thought," said Gubblebum, "Oh look, I think I can see my friend...yes it is...it's Amanda Salad and she's got the baby. Oh I do hope he's not been too much trouble...he's teething you see."

"Aye it can be the verra devil...I mind when Cuddly was cutting her teeth oor mither never got a wink of sleep for days on end."

Gubblebum thought of the rows of sharp-pointed teeth that stretched like park-railings and her heart went out to Mrs Sea-Serpent. Gubblebum propelled the two bubbles up to the beach and with a wave of her hands magicked them away. She ran up the beach to where Amanda Salad stood looking down at the baby with a soppy look on her face. Pancake raced up the sand, scampered around the two witches barking madly then he spotted a rabbit hopping peacefully along one of the sand-dunes and he was off.

"Has he been alright?" asked Gubblebum anxiously.

"He's been good as gold haven't oo iddums widdums?" Auntie Mandy-Pandy's given you a bottle and changed your little bottie-wottie and now oo's all clean and cuddly isn't oo diddums?"

Gubblebum started to feel angry. "Rolly do you mean to say I've been away for days and you've only fed him and changed him once?"

Amanda Salad looked worried, hurt and puzzled all at the same time...which isn't easy.

"Days Gubble? You only set off to find out about those dreadful sea-serpents this morning... it looks as if you found one of them at least."

"This morning?!" muttered Gubblebum. Then she realised that time in the world under the sea passes much quicker than it does on land hence the old saying, "Time flies when you're having fins!"

"Is that one of them?" asked Amanda Salad.

"One of what?"

"The sea-serpents who are causing all the damage here in Baywitch?"

"It's a long story Rolly. Let's go and have a nice cup of Witche's Brew and I'll tell you all about it." She turned to the sea and cupping her hands to her mouth she shouted to Loch Ness, "Don't go away. We're just going for a cuppa... we'd ask you to join us but Rolly's cottage is rather small and you are... well... longish."

The sea-serpent laughed. "Aye yer right there lassie haggis ah am at that. Dinna fret yersel' aboot me ah'll just paddle aboot here and admire the scenery... makes a nice change after being stuck in that lake all this time."

Over a nice steaming cup of tea Gubblebum told Amanda Salad all her adventures on the bottom of the ocean.

"Tonight we'll go down to the beach and watch the sea-serpents' reunion... should be worth staying up for."

Baywitch beach lay silver under a bright moon as Amanda Salad and Gubblebum carrying the baby who was snug in his sleep-suit decorated with broomsticks, cauldrons and pointy hats sleeping like... well like a baby. The sea stretched like a huge mirror. Its surface was broken only by the eight

125

rounded humps of Loch-Ness as she waited for her sisters.

Like children wriggling under the bed clothes, four swirling lumps appeared on the ocean's smooth surface. Then the humps grew and grew and came swishing towards the beach and the two witches. Out of the shimmering water rose four huge heads which swung ponderously around then stopped. It is hard to imagine... (so I'm not going to try...) what a sea-serpent looks like when it's surprised, especially in moonlight. However, there was no doubt as to the joy when the four sea-serpents saw their long-lost sister. Such a swirling, twisting and coiling has never been seen before or since.

The calm sea was thrashed into foam as the giant creatures leapt and gambolled. Gubblebum and Amanda

Salad had to run back up the beach as waves came roaring and crashing onto the sand. One especially large wave almost toppled the Hot Dog van which had been rescued from the hole made by the sea-serpent's foot.

All at once the turmoil in the sea stopped and the two witches saw all five of the sea-serpents gazing intently at the horizon where a red glow had spread to cover the sky.

"Rolly, I know time's been acting funny recently but surely it can't be dawn yet," said Gubblebum.

"It isn't... Gubble - look!" whispered Amanda Salad. At first Gubblebum thought it was a giant thundercloud which was filling the entire sky but she heard a high-pitched sighing noise and saw that an immense extra-terrestrial craft was approaching the

Baywitch beach. The sighing noise died away and the gigantic craft hung over the witches and the five sea-serpents. As if a switch had been thrown, a cone of dazzling blue light covered the five sisters. As quickly as it had come it disappeared and when the witches looked again the sea-serpents were gone.

A red glow, a sighing and the black cloud which was the U.F.O. began to move slowly away then a voice came echoing through the air.

"Ta ta Gubblebum ma wee lassie...we can never thank ye enough for what ye've done fer us. We'll never forget ye... oh, by the by, ye were asking what the five of us were called well most fowk where we come from call us the Space Girls...Goodbye!"

The following morning Gubblebum had loaded all her gear... and the baby's... (She was seriously thinking of a trip to Meadow-Spell for extra bristles) onto the broomstick. She gave her friend a hug and a kiss saying, "Well thanks for everything Rolly, it's been a lovely couple of days... just what I needed to liven me up again." She grinned, "Thanks for looking after iddum-diddums here."

She gazed fondly at the baby who was energetically trying to separate Pancake from his tail. Amanda Salad's eyes took on that soppy dreamy look and she blushed.

"Rolly! You're holding out on me... come on, who is he?"

"Well Gubble while you were away I was using a bit of magic... only low-grade stuff to help tidy up the beach and I sort of levitated Derek's Hot Dog Stall out of that sea-serpent print and... oh Gubble he's so nice and... er... well... nice."

Gubblebum hugged her friend again, "I must say Rolly it's not before time... don't forget to send us an invitation to the wedding...I'll call you soon...Bye!" With a throaty roar the G.T.I. broomstick lifted into the sky....

Well that's about it really. Calvin was back from his opening, cutting and shaking tour with Walter... his hands were a bit sore but he made some fantastic balloon-animals at Princess Gravelinetta's second birthday party.
The five multi-coloured sea-serpents were a work of art.

That's the end of my tale and Pancake's... oh I forgot to tell you - he's started coming back from his forest outings soaking wet. Gubblebum suspects that after his undersea adventures he's started chasing fish as well as rabbits!

THE END

HE...HE...EH...EH...EH

That still doesn't sound very evil does it? Who knows, perhaps Amanda Salad will send us an invitation to the wedding...we'll have to wait and sea...I mean see! Bye!

"Words Free Us All"

Congratulations Rhino Readers, you've finished the book.
Mission Accomplished!

We hope you enjoyed your reading journey and would love to
know how you found it.

Got any feedback, comments or criticisms? Spotted a typo or
want to leave a review?

Visit our website www.stormrhinopublishing.com

or email us at feedback@stormrhinopublishing.com